The Moffats

The Middle Moffat

Rufus M.

The Sun and the Wind and Mr. Todd

The Hundred Dresses

The Sleeping Giant

Ginger Pye
(Newbery Medal Winner)

A Little Oven

Pinky Pye

The Witch Family

The Alley

Miranda the Great

The Lollipop Princess

The Tunnel of Hugsy Goode

The Coat-Hanger
Christmas Tree

The Coat-Hanger
Christmas Tree

Eleanor Estes

Illustrated by Susanne Suba

A MARGARET K. MC ELDERRY BOOK

Atheneum   *1973*   *New York*

To Lydia

Contents

The Coat-Hanger
Christmas Tree

Marianna

IT WAS DARK when Marianna left school and started for home. Only four-thirty and dark already! Tomorrow was the twenty-first of December, the shortest day of the year for everybody, but even shorter for children at school because at noontime, after singing carols and watching Mr. Mitchner be Santa Claus as he was every year, school would be over and Christmas vacation would start.

Marianna was almost ten. She was not afraid to walk home alone. The shops were brightly lighted and many houses, too, some with Christmas trees in their windows. Still it would have been nicer to walk home with her brother, Kenny. Kenny was eleven and in room six. She was in room five and, along with a few other children, she had stayed late to help Miss Bogan trim the tree.

Maybe Kenny had stayed late for the same reason. Every single room in P.S. 9 had a small Christmas tree in it. There was also a huge tree in the assembly hall for the Christmas program tomorrow. Maybe Kenny was helping to trim that one. Or maybe he was already home.

She couldn't go to Kenny's room or to the assembly hall to find out if he were still at school because the janitor in his gray-striped denim overalls said, "Everybody out—everybody go home." And he practically swept her and her classmates out the door with his big bristly broom. In fun. The minute he opened the heavy front door that children only used when they stayed late, Marianna's classmates all disappeared. They were hungry, probably. "Smell like pine?"

You could understand Allie McKaye disappearing as fast as that, because Allie was always running, always in a rush, with her long green coat flapping around her ankles and her head thrust forward like the prow of a ship. But the other children weren't usually so speedy.

Marianna walked slowly. She was in no hurry to get home where, so far, there was no sign of Christmas. It was a misty evening, not too cold, and maybe it would snow later. It usually did snow for Christmas, Marianna thought happily. There were Christmas trees everywhere. Their fragrance filled the air. Marianna breathed deeply. She opened her mouth and swallowed a mouthful of the pine-scented air. "Smell my breath," she'd say to Kenny when she got home.

In the bay a buoy went bong . . . bong . . . a slow and giant metronome for the muffled sound of foghorns on the boats and the barges. A lighted tanker headed out to sea. For this was in Brooklyn, down near the water, where ships from Japan came in, and from Chile, and where barges tied up too and unloaded their cargo. Marianna's tall brownstone house was just a few blocks away. She could hear all these sounds of the harbor from it and the screaming of the gulls, which sometimes lighted on her roof on a stormy day. She could smell the coffee and spices carried by the ships, and chocolate from a nearby

candy factory, and bread being baked in shops on Atlantic Avenue.

She missed Kenny. She and Kenny almost always walked home from school together. They'd stop and look through the doors and windows of the shops to see the huge kegs of ripe olives, the stacks of flat round loaves of Syrian bread, and the sweets that made their mouths water—baklava and honey cakes. On the way home she and Kenny talked about everything. But today what Marianna wanted to talk about was trees—Christmas trees.

Some of the empty, boarded-up stores had been opened and were selling Christmas trees. And in empty lots there were stacks of them tied together with brown rope. Imagine all these trees! And back in school, in P.S. 9, imagine all those. Yet tomorrow when Christmas vacation began, the trees in school would be taken down and put out in the street to be carted away.

Marianna turned the corner. She left Atlantic Avenue behind with its bright lights and stores and people and new trees, and now she was on a street where there was a small college. At the curbing a Christmas tree was lying, not a new one. Marianna stopped and studied the abandoned tree. Somebody had had this tree up, had trimmed it, and had sung songs around it perhaps; and they had already taken it down and put it outside, and it wasn't even Christmas yet. Like the trees at school, it would be carted away tomorrow, too.

"It probably belonged to some college boy," Marianna thought. "He probably had a party in his room last night, and then today he took his tree down because he had to go away somewhere, far away somewhere for his vacation."

There were bits of silver icicles still on the tree. "This tree is just the right size for our house," Marianna thought. "Not too big, not too small." It was still fresh and crisp, not dried out. Marianna picked up a small twig that had broken off and put it in her buttonhole, the top one so she could smell it. At home, in her room, she had a sturdy little pillow filled with pine needles. It had a brown pine cone painted on the outside of it. Her Aunt Lyddy had sent it to her from Lebanon, Maine. It had come through the mail with her name, Marianna Lamb, and her address, 9 Pine Street, Brooklyn, New York, on a little tag tied to it. It wasn't even wrapped up, but it had come safely. She kept it on her bed beside her real pillow because she liked to smell it.

Marianna couldn't bear to leave this still-good Christmas tree that had been thrown away and was lying here. In her house they had never had a Christmas tree. Every Christmas she and her brother Kenny asked their mother why—why they couldn't have a Christmas tree. "Please, this year, let's have a Christmas tree, Mama," they begged. "Please, Mama, please!"

"No," their mother said every time.

"Why?" they asked. "Why can't we have a Christmas tree? Just tell us a reason."

"Because," their mother said, "I don't believe in doing something just because a million other people do it. See? Now just don't nag at me any more about trees."

Marianna and Kenny always wished their father would put in a word for them—like, "Oh, go ahead, Adelaide. Let the children have a tree." But he never did. He was away right now on a long journey studying for a book he was going to write on tropical architecture. But even if he were home, he wouldn't say that. He always left the customs of the house up to their mother. Have a tree, not have a tree; believe in Santa Claus, not believe in Santa Claus; go trick or treating on Hallowe'en, not go trick or treating—they never did; believe in the Easter bunny, not believe in the Easter bunny: all these customs depended on their mother, and she didn't go for any of them. She just didn't like the idea of seeming to be like everybody else. She liked to be "different."

Yet once, Marianna mused, their mother had made an Easter egg tree. She liked to make things, and they all had fun together painting the eggs and hanging them up. It was pretty. So Marianna and Kenny never gave up hope about having a Christmas tree. What was the sense of a person who would make an Easter egg tree but wouldn't let them have a Christmas tree? Marianna and Kenny often puzzled about this, but they never found an answer.

Now, Marianna stooped over and picked up the abandoned Christmas tree. She stood it upright. It was about six feet high. She couldn't bear to put it back down and leave it. She looked all around her. Some of the windows in the houses had lighted Christmas trees in them. Those trees were in the houses of the kind of people who put their tree up before Christmas. Marianna knew other people who put their tree up late, on Christmas Eve, after the children had gone to bed. Then, early in the morning when the children raced downstairs with cold bare feet—behold! there the tree would be, all lighted, as though brought by magic in the middle of the night by Santa Claus. "O-o-oh!" they would gasp, and stand and look.

Marianna had some friends whose parents went by the first custom and others who went by the second. There were some arguments about which custom was better. If Marianna could have a choice, she would choose the second way, having the tree brought by magic in the middle of the night, all trimmed and shining with lights.

But she couldn't choose either of these nice customs because of the custom in her house of never having a tree at all. She stood beside the abandoned tree and pondered. What a nice shape it had . . . it was perfect. Why not take it home? She and Kenny could trim it together. That's what she would do. She'd take it home. Her mother could stay out of the room where it was until after Christmas.

Marianna went on some steps, holding the tree upright. She and the tree took up the whole sidewalk. People had to walk around her. If anyone said, "Hey. What are you doing, lugging away that Christmas tree?" she'd say, "It's not stealing to take a Christmas tree that someone has thrown away."

She trudged along another few paces. If Kenny were with her, he could not only help her carry the tree, he could also stand up for her when she showed it to her mother. When her mother saw this tree that was in her own house, she might suddenly, seeing how pretty it was, change her mind right then and there. She might say, "Oh, O.K. then. Let's keep the tree. It's nice." She might like it, not say it was foolishness, not mind being like every tom-dick-and-harry. Sometimes people do change their minds, even people who are very set on some idea.

Just lately, she, herself—Marianna—had changed her mind about something. At first she had agreed with a boy who said he didn't like Allie McKaye. She said she didn't either. One day she asked that boy— his name was Pete Calahan—why he didn't like Allie McKaye, why he kept grabbing her hat off and throwing it someplace where she couldn't get it. Pete said he just plain didn't like her, that's all. Anyway, he said, Allie wasn't in school long enough at a time for him to get used to the idea of her. She'd be in school for a week or two and then she'd be away for a week or two. How can you get to like a stranger that way?

Marianna decided that was a silly reason for not liking Allie McKaye. So she changed her mind about her. She began to like Allie, and she ate her sandwich with her in the lunchroom. The times when Allie was away she missed her, she was lonesome for her. She really liked Allie McKaye, the way she ran, for instance.

So . . . her mother might get the idea that her reason for not having a Christmas tree was silly, too. She might think, "Hey. What's the matter with me? It's not the people that have the trees that are foolish, it's me." She'd laugh at herself, then. Everybody would laugh. And now, when she saw this tree that Marianna was bringing home—it was harder to manage than she had thought, and she had scratched her cheek—her mother would say, "It's just about time we had a Christmas tree in this house! Come on. Hurry up in. You're freezing out the house!"

The little street Marianna was walking on now was very dark except for the lights in the windows and the street lamps. She stood the tree upright on the sidewalk and rested. It was quiet on this street. In the quiet she heard someone running behind her. She couldn't hide herself altogether behind her tree, but it was comforting to have it with her since Kenny wasn't.

"I won't be frightened," Marianna told herself. "I won't be scared. I'll stand still behind my tree, not run."

She stood stock still, scarcely breathing. And the running steps came closer. Marianna circled halfway around the tree, and she looked to see who the person was. It was Allie McKaye in her long green coat, about to run past her.

"Hi!" said Marianna coming out from behind the tree. "Wait, Allie. Wait!"

Allie McKaye

ALLIE STOPPED short. She smiled when she saw Marianna. "Hi!" she said. She had a gentle, shy, rather high-pitched voice.

"Where are you going?" asked Marianna. "I didn't know you lived near me."

"I don't," said Allie. Then she quickly changed the subject. "I have to go to the store for my mother," she said. "Is that going to be your Christmas tree?"

"I hope so," said Marianna. "But I don't know. I don't know whether my mother will say O.K. or not. We never have had a Christmas tree in my house."

"You haven't!" said Allie.

"No," said Marianna. There was a pause. Before Allie could run away, Marianna added hastily, "Well, if you don't live around here, where do you live?"

Allie was silent. After a while she said, "I'll tell you tomorrow."

"Why don't you tell me now?" Marianna persisted. "Is it anywhere near me? I live on Pine Street, number nine Pine Street. Maybe we could play together some day during vacation."

"No," said Allie. She took a deep breath. "I live on a barge," she said.

"A barge!" Marianna exclaimed. "O-o-oh, that must be great! I didn't know girls—people—lived on barges. I just didn't know that. It must be fun!"

"I hate it," said Allie.

"Why?" asked Marianna incredulously. "To live on a boat! My!"

"I hate it," said Allie. "I don't have a bureau. I don't have any bureau with drawers to keep things in . . . to keep handkerchiefs in, ironed, folded up in a little stack . . . I . . ."

And Allie ran away, her green coat flapping against her shins, her head thrust forward and uptilted as though it would get there, to where she was running, long before the rest of her.

"What'd she run away for?" Marianna wondered. Astonished, she watched Allie as long as she could see her. She saw what a sensible coat her long green maxi coat was. Allie could unzip the bottom part of the coat and take it off when it was warm. Then she could zip it back on again when it grew cold. How nice and snug it must be when cutting winds blew across the barge!

All of a sudden Allie came running back. "Don't tell anyone at school I live on a barge," she said. "Don't tell Pete Calahan. Promise!"

"Can't I tell my own brother? Kenny?" asked Marianna.

"Well . . . just him, then. But make him promise not to tell anyone else . . . not Pete Calahan, he hates me." And Allie ran away again.

"I wish she wouldn't run away," thought Marianna. "I wish she'd ask me to come and play with her on her barge. A bureau isn't that important, is it? Well, it must be important to her like—like this Christmas tree, any Christmas tree, is important to me. That's right."

She hoisted her tree over her shoulder. There were only two more short blocks to go on this street. Then she'd turn the corner into her own street, Pine Street, and her house was the second on the left, number nine.

By the time she reached her corner, she was tired. She stood the tree against a lamppost and rubbed her hands. They would have had blisters on them by now if it had not been for the bright red mittens her Aunt Lyddy in Lebanon, Maine, had knitted for her.

There, in Maine, they had so many evergreen trees . . . pines, firs, hemlocks, spruce, balsam! Her Aunt Lyddy didn't see why Marianna couldn't have a Christmas tree. Once she wrote that in a letter to Marianna's mother, but she never wrote it again. They just didn't agree about trees . . . Marianna's mother and her Aunt Lyddy.

Marianna stood at the corner and looked at her tall narrow house. It was one room wide and three rooms deep and three stories high plus a cellar. It was a pretty house. None would look prettier than it with a Christmas tree in the middle front window . . . lighted up and trimmed.

The lights in her house were on downstairs. The rest of the house was dark, including the third floor where her bedroom was. Her bedroom was perfect. She could see the water from way up there, see the boats and bridges and barges tied up at piers or being tugged somewhere. All the times that she had looked out of her window and seen a barge she had never had the least idea that a girl the same age as herself in her same class in school, Allie McKaye, lived on one.

She didn't have a bureau, Allie didn't. She probably didn't have a

Christmas tree either. Marianna had never heard of a Christmas tree on a barge. Probably there were lots of things about living on a barge that she had never heard of or even thought to think about.

Marianna picked up her tree for the final lap home. Suddenly her front door opened and light flooded the stoop. Was it her mother? Marianna kept on walking. What she was going to say was, "Don't hurt this Christmas tree. Don't throw it away. It's my tree I found . . . my Christmas tree . . . *our* Christmas tree. Let's put it up. Please, Mama, please."

But it wasn't her mother, it was Kenny. He had seen her coming from the window. Not waiting to put on a coat, he rushed out to help her. "Hey!" he said. "Where'd you get that tree? Did you meet Mama? Did she buy it and give it to you to bring home? That's not fair. I wish I could have gone with you to pick out the tree. Our first tree! What made her change her mind? Did you meet her on Atlantic Avenue?"

"No," said Marianna. "I didn't see Mama. She doesn't know anything about the tree yet. I found the tree. Near the college. Somebody had thrown it away, just thrown it away. So I brought it home."

"All by yourself?" asked Kenny.

"All by myself." Marianna smiled proudly.

"It's a beauty," said Kenny. "It sure is a beauty. But I don't think Mama will let you keep it. Don't get your hopes up."

"Don't say that," said Marianna. She was tired, and she was almost crying.

"Oh, O.K." said Kenny. "Come on. Hurry up. We'll put it out in the garden before Mama comes in."

Since their house was one of a row of connected houses, they had to go through the house to get to the garden. They pulled the tree through the front door, the large trunk end first not to snap off branches, through the house, and out the back door. There was a high brick wall at the back of the garden, and they leaned the tree in a corner against it. It was so dark out that, standing at the kitchen door, if you didn't know there was a tree there, you wouldn't notice it. The sky was a dark gray, but in the west the lights of the city cast a soft glow.

Marianna and Kenny closed the back door and went through the house to the narrow front parlor. This room had three windows facing the street, and they looked out of the one on the right, waiting and watching for their mother.

"Did Mama take the baby with her?" Marianna asked.

The baby's name was Roderick, and he was seven months old.

"No," said Kenny. "He's asleep upstairs, and I'm minding him. That's why I didn't go to meet you. I wondered why you were so late."

"I stayed after school to help Miss Bogan trim the tree," said Marianna. "Some other kids stayed, too. Allie McKaye stayed. You know Allie McKaye?"

". . . she that girl that's always running? That always wears that long green coat?" asked Kenny.

"Yeh. Well . . . guess where she lives," said Marianna.

"I don't know . . . where?" asked Kenny.

"You'll never guess in one thousand years," said Marianna. "She lives on a barge, Kenny. She lives on a barge, right on the water!"

"Hey!" said Kenny. "That's great! Do you know the name of it?"

"No," said Marianna. "That's all she said. She lives on a barge, she said, and then she ran away. Then she came back, and she said not to tell anybody. And I said could I tell you, and she said yes, but not to tell anybody else at school, not to tell Pete Calahan especially."

Kenny smiled. He felt happy and important to be one of the few people in the world who knew this secret about where a girl named Allie McKaye lived.

Marianna said, "Maybe . . . maybe she'll invite me to visit her some day on her barge."

"Get her to invite me, too," said Kenny. "You know her barge might be one of those tied up at the pier at the end of our street. Let's go up to your room and look at them," he said. "Sh-sh-sh! Don't wake the baby."

They tiptoed up to Marianna's room and looked out of her bay window over the roof tops of the houses beyond. Sure enough, they could see dark barges tied to the wharves and other ships at other piers, festooned with lights, made pretty for the holidays.

One barge also had colored lights on it. Through the mist they looked like lights on a Christmas tree—that was the shape the lights made, the shape of a Christmas tree.

"Hey," said Marianna. "That sure looks like a Christmas tree on that barge down there, the one that's farthest out on the pier!"

"You're right," said Kenny. "It does! You'd think the wind would blow it into the water."

"There's not much wind out now," said Marianna. "But—imagine a Christmas tree on a barge! Still, if a girl can live on a barge, anything can be on a barge . . . a Christmas tree . . . a birthday party . . . anything . . ." She already felt staunch and loyal to her new friend and proud of her. "If Allie thinks it's terrible to live on a barge, you must not tell one soul," said Marianna. "I promised her."

"Of course, I won't," said Kenny.

"You know what?" Marianna said. "That barge with the tree on it might be hers. I'll ask her tomorrow."

Across the bay the Manhattan skyscrapers were ablaze with lights, and the lights on the bridges that spanned the East River looked like sparkling necklaces. "Kenny, the city is like a giant Christmas tree," Marianna said. "The bridges are the branches, and you know what we are? A decoration at the end of the long branch that is the Brooklyn Bridge. The island of Manhattan is the trunk of the tree . . ."

"The star at the top of the trunk, if we could see it, could be the North star," said Kenny.

"And the boats and the barges are toys under the tree," said Marianna.

"Right," said Kenny. "Hey, get the name of the barge of that girl that you know. . . ."

"Allie McKaye," said Marianna.

"Yes," said Kenny. "Get the name of her barge, and some day when we take a walk down the pier, we'll look for it."

"O.K.," said Marianna. "I hope it's the one with the tree. But now we better go downstairs and let Mama in when she comes home. She might have lots of packages . . . even a tree. Who knows?"

"A tree! Ha-ha!" said Kenny.

The First Tree

BACK DOWNSTAIRS at the front window, Marianna and Kenny pressed their noses against the glass, shielded their eyes with their hands, and peered out. They thought they saw their mother coming, but it was a neighbor, Mrs. Alysius, smiling and waving. "Got your tree yet?" she shouted. She was quite deaf and did not expect to hear an answer even if the window had been open.

Marianna smiled back at her and nodded her head up and down and that meant yes, they did have a tree. Mrs. Alysius waved a branch of holly at them and went busily up the street. "She's forgotten we never have a tree," Kenny said.

"But we do have a tree," said Marianna. "It's true."

"We have a bare abandoned tree in the back yard. But we don't have a real Christmas tree until Mama sees it, says, 'Great! Bring it in,' " said Kenny gloomily.

Marianna was determined not to let her spirits sag. "Kenny," she said. "We have to be just as set on having a tree as Mama is on not having a tree."

"Well, anyway," Kenny said. "Here she comes now. Here Mama comes, and now we'll know."

Their mother had her boots on, and her coat collar was pulled up high around her neck. She had two huge brown bags, one under each arm. Celery stalks stuck out of one bag, and a long loaf of bread out of the other. Rapt in her thoughts, she did not notice her children waiting at the window and didn't wave.

Marianna and Kenny ran to the door and opened it so she would not have to get out her key. They studied her face, and her face didn't tell them anything. Even if it had been cross, it would not have been so because Marianna had brought a Christmas tree home and put it in the garden. Mama couldn't know about that yet. If her face were cross, it would have been for some other reason—perhaps because she had not had a letter from Papa for two weeks: "This holiday mail!" she'd say. "This Post Office!" or perhaps because she thought the man in the fruit store had tried to cheat her again, or . . . because of anything. . . .

"Hi, everybody," she said. Then she said, "Who dragged in all these pine needles all over the house? Can't you wipe your feet before you come in?" She went into the kitchen with her packages and put them on the table. "Tracked these needles way in here," she said. "Somebody get the dustpan and brush them up . . . Is the baby still asleep?"

"Yes," Marianna said.

Their mother went upstairs to tend to the baby. Marianna swept up the pine needles. "When Mama comes down, I'll tell her about the tree," she said.

"Maybe you should wait," said Kenny. "She's a little cross now . . . about the pine needles. We should have thought to sweep them up."

"Well," Marianna said. "I'll see. If a good chance comes, like—when we're all laughing at the baby, then I'll say it, maybe. I'll say 'We have a tree, Mama.' "

Their mother came downstairs with the baby and put him in a little half-reclining seat on the dining room table where he could see everything and everybody. She gave him his bottle, and she looked down at him smiling. She didn't look the least bit cross. "Children are best at this stage . . . the baby stage . . ." she said.

For a second Marianna almost wished she was a baby again herself.

She stood beside the baby and looked down at him, and he looked up at her, took his bottle out of his mouth, smiled in ecstasy, and suddenly hurled his bottle away. Marianna caught it and gave it back to him.

"No, no!" she said. "Bad baby. Mustn't do that. Mustn't always try to throw your bottle away."

The baby gurgled, said "Coo!" and plopped his bottle back in his mouth. Marianna stood by in case he'd give it another pitch.

"Mama," Marianna said. "You know what? I bet the baby would just love a Christmas tree . . . the pretty lights on it . . . the balls he'd see himself and everything reflected in . . . the pine smell of it. I bet he'd laugh and clap his hands every minute we had the tree up and never cry and never have colic . . . just always squeal and gurgle and say, 'Coo,' and give speeches in his language."

"He says 'coo' plenty often enough to suit me," their mother said. "And he makes plenty of long speeches—he'll be a politician at this rate."

She chucked him under the chin. He took his bottle out of his mouth and said, "Coo," again. "See?" she said. "We don't need Christmas trees and all that stuff to get him to coo more. He's going to be brought up the same way as both of you, the same way exactly," she said.

"But everybody has a Christmas tree!" Marianna shouted angrily. "Even Allie McKaye—she's a girl in my class who lives on a barge—I bet even she has a tree! Kenny and me, we just now saw a barge with a Christmas tree lighted on it. I bet it was hers. I bet it was Allie's barge. I'm going to ask her tomorrow."

"A Christmas tree between the crates of coal," their mother said. "Tell that to the marines!" The idea amused her and she laughed.

"I bet she does . . . I bet she does . . ." Marianna stormed. Her voice broke, she couldn't say another word. The baby hurled his bottle across the room. This time Kenny caught it.

"Neat catch," said their mother. "But, so what? Even if people who live on barges go in for Christmas trees, is that any reason for us to, too? You don't have to have everybody growing up exactly alike, do you, all doing exactly the same thing, do you? We're not going to begin having Christmas trees in this house just because every tom-and-dick-and-harriet, including that whatser name on a barge, has one . . . if she does. I never in all my born days heard of a stupider reason . . . thought you all had more sense . . ."

She picked the baby up and hugged him for a minute, and she burped him and put him back down. He began to stare unblinkingly at a mobile of little fish his mother had made for him and hung from the ceiling. He was absorbed and quite thoughtful.

Marianna grew calm and thoughtful too. "That's so pretty, that mobile is," she said. "You make such pretty things, Mama. You . . . we . . . could all make pretty things for the tree. We have lots of time left to make lots of things because tomorrow is the last day of school. We could bake cookies, cinnamon cookies in the shapes of animals and stars and gingerbread boys, put raisins in for the eyes, thread them, and hang them on the tree . . . give one to everybody who comes in to see our tree . . ." she said.

"Yeh," said Kenny. "We can make cornucopias and fill them with popcorn . . ."

"And chains out of old wallpaper—there's some in the attic—link circles of it together and wind the chains around the tree," said Marianna.

"Get some lights," said Kenny. "String them around . . ."

"M-m-m," their mother said absent-mindedly, as she went into the kitchen to prepare dinner.

Then Kenny shouted. "We just can't see why—if we paint Easter eggs and even had an egg tree once, remember?—why we can't make Christmas tree ornaments and have a Christmas tree! What's the difference? Where's the sense?"

"An egg tree is more unusual . . . you don't get every tom-dick-and-harry making egg trees." Mama turned on the radio. "Now stop harping on Christmas trees, will you? I want to hear the news . . . Saturday we'll all go downtown to the big stores, and you can see the mess they have there they call trees! All covered with balls. You don't even know if there's a tree underneath them at all . . . the whole thing might be made out of, out of . . . coat-hangers or some other gol-durn thing."

"Well, we don't have to trim our tree at all, then," said Marianna. "If that's what you don't like. We can just leave it nice and green and fir-y if you are against lots of balls . . . if that's all that's the matter . . . even if Kenny and me . . . we do like trimmings, don't we, Kenny? Anyway, Mama. You know what?" Marianna's voice shook a little, but she went on. "I—we, Kenny and me—already have a tree, a Christmas tree, just plain and green. Just a plain pine tree. It's in the garden."

Her mother stirred what she was cooking.

"Did you hear me, Mama?" Marianna spoke loudly. No one could help but hear her, even above the news on WOR. "I have a tree!"

"Sh-sh-sh," said her mother. "They're giving the weather."

"I know what the weather is. Come on, Mama. Come and look out the back door, Mama," Marianna said. "You'll see the weather, and you'll see my Christmas tree." She grabbed her mother's hand, pulled her to the door, and opened it. "There," she said. "There's my Christmas tree, Mama. Do you see it? Do you like it?"

"Hm-m-m," her mother said. "I see it all right. And that's where it's going to stay." She went back to the stove to stir the dinner, and that was all she said.

Suddenly Marianna felt happy. Now her mother knew about the tree. She hadn't gotten cross, and she hadn't made Marianna drag the tree back through the house and throw it away or done the same herself. True, she hadn't said, "Good!" or "Hooray!" But the tree was still there.

Marianna went into the dining room and whispered in the baby's ear. "We're going to have a tree, yes, we are." This made the baby laugh. Marianna stroked his cheek. "You're a sweet baby," she said.

"Oh, stop calling him 'baby,'" her mother said. "He has a name—Roderick. Everybody call him Roderick."

"You call him 'baby' yourself," Kenny said.

"I know it. Not any more, though. He's growing up. From now on everybody call him Roderick," his mother said.

"Roderick!" Marianna said. "Could I call him 'Roddie'?"

"Or 'Rod'?" asked Kenny.

"No. I'm tired of nicknames. I never did like being called 'Addie.' I've decided, no more nicknames. Call the baby 'Roderick.' He's named after my grandfather . . . Grandfather Roderick," she said. "And you, Kendrick . . ."

"Kendrick!" exclaimed Marianna.

"Yes, Kendrick," her mother said. "I've decided. No more of this 'Kenny' business. From now on it's Kendrick."

"I'm not going to tell the kids at school," said Kenny. "Kendrick!

Who'm I named after?"

"You forget everything. You're named after my other grandfather—Grandfather Kendrick. A pillar of the church! Who would ever have said 'Grampa Kenny'?"

"Whee-ee!" said Marianna. "I'm glad my name is Marianna. Who'm I named after?"

"Your grandmother. That is—my mother. She died when I was a baby. On Christmas Eve."

"On Christmas E-eeve!" said Marianna.

"Yes," her mother said. "That's what my dad told me."

"Christmas Eve," said Marianna again. She stood stock still, stunned as though she had had a terrible blow on her head. She looked at her mother as though she saw her for the first time. She'd never really looked at her mother before. She took in her face, round and rather flat with great gray eyes, took in her hair, straight and brown and short, took in the lines by her mouth, which turned up on one side and down on the other, took in her red sweater and blue jeans.

Suddenly she felt she didn't know her mother at all. She felt the way she had once when, not expecting to see her, she came upon her in the museum the day Marianna's class was visiting it. That time she had had this same funny feeling of knowing, yet not knowing her mother. Her heart had pounded. She didn't want to speak to her. She had pretended she had not seen her. She was awfully familiar and awfully strange at the same time . . . just like now, when Marianna had learned for the first time that *her* mother had died on Christmas Eve.

It was a scary feeling. Supposing her mother—Mama—should die on Christmas Eve. What would she do? She was frightened. She wanted to run to her mother and hold her, say, "Don't die on Christmas Eve, Mama. Don't die. Don't die ever." But she was rooted to the floor and watched her mother do things for the baby in a daze. Then she shook her head as though she had come up from a deep dive. She saw her mother the way she always saw her—that is, not really seeing her at all, her mother being just her regular mother, not a stranger in a museum, and yet—not quite the same regular mother. The difference was that now she knew that, when she was a baby, this regular mother's own mother had died on Christmas Eve, and Marianna had never known one thing about that until right now.

After dinner she and Kenny went up to her room and looked out of her window, the way they did every evening before they went to bed.

"Did you hear what Mama said?" she asked Kenny, edging close to him. "That her mother died on Christmas Eve?"

"Yeh," said Kenny. "But that was a long time ago, a long, long time ago. It doesn't have anything to do with right now, with you and me."

"That's right," said Marianna. "That's right," she said, relieved.

The Shoe-Box Room

KENNY WENT to his room to read. For a while Marianna didn't turn on her light. She looked out at the water, the bridges, and the skyline mysteriously beautiful behind the soft snow falling now. Somewhere down there, beside some dock, was the barge where Allie McKaye lived. Marianna wondered if Allie had a bunk in a cozy little room below the hatches, like a cabin on a regular boat, that was always nice and warm.

Many boats in the bay were decorated with lights from stem to stern. But Marianna was searching for the barge that she and Kenny thought had a Christmas tree on it. There it was—she saw it now—with its Christmas tree lights, tied up at Pier 16. Marianna was impatient for tomorrow to come so she could say to Allie, "Is that your barge at Pier 16 that has a Christmas tree on it?"

Imagine living on a barge that had a lighted Christmas tree on deck! Marianna could not stop marveling at the idea. At last she turned on her light and sat down at her desk. She kept thinking about Allie and how she hated living on the barge. "I know what," she thought. "I'll

make her a Christmas present and give it to her tomorrow in school—
a good luck present."

Everyone in Marianna's family liked to make things. They made most
of the presents they gave to each other and their friends. The cellar was
the best place to make things in—all the tools were there. But the present Marianna was going to make for Allie could be made right up here
in her own room. It was going to be a miniature copy of her room,
bureau and all.

Marianna got a shoe box out of her closet that she usually kept her
best shoes in. Like her room it was light blue. It was going to be a miniature bedroom for Allie. She made a small bed, a rocking chair, a
little bureau, and a desk . . . all out of cardboard. She stuck the pieces

together with Elmer's glue. She wanted to fix the bureau so the drawers could be pulled in and out. It was not too hard to do because she made the drawers out of little empty matchboxes she had saved. Finally she got everything to work—the chair to rock, the drawers to open and close—but it was fragile. It had to be handled with care.

Then she cut tiny squares out of an old white sheet for handkerchiefs. She folded them up and stacked them in a pile in the top matchbox drawer. She painted a bookcase on one wall with different colored books in it and with the names of some of the books she and Kenny loved the most. *Floating Island* was one, and she thought that the barge with the tree on it, which she hoped was Allie's, was very much like a floating island.

After that, she went downstairs and got the pine tree twig from the buttonhole of her coat. She made it stand up in a corner of the shoe-box room between the bureau and the window, and now the room had a tree. She strung tiny colored beads into garlands and wound them around the tree, and she made a two-by-three inch rug out of red worsted and put it on the floor beside the bed. She was finished. The shoe-box room looked very pretty.

Feeling happy, Marianna began to get ready for bed. She took a last look out of her window. All the lights were blurred by the hazy snow. "It's like a dream," thought Marianna. Now and then boats whistled, some hurriedly, worriedly . . . others slowly, deeply, reassuringly. All these sounds put Marianna to sleep every night, and she loved them.

Before hopping into bed, she tiptoed to the little back bedroom where Kenny slept, along with all his fish in tanks and his two gerbils named Pezda and Mezda. He was still reading. They looked down into the garden. They could see their tree—fluffy snow outlining its shape.

"It's still there," said Marianna happily.

"Yes," said Kenny. "But don't get your hopes up, Marianna. You know Mama. She won't change her mind about a tree. She just likes to be different, likes not to be the same as everybody else, likes not to do the same things most people do . . ."

"Well, anyway," said Marianna. "I'm going to keep right on thinking she will let us bring my tree in and trim it, maybe *help* us trim it. To-morrow, while we are at school, she'll probably get used to the whole idea. When we get home, she'll probably say, 'Well . . . what's the good of a Christmas tree out there in the garden? Bring it in, you dopes, so we can trim it.' "

"Bedtime," their mother called up the stairs. "Aren't you in bed yet?"

Marianna ran back to her room. "Yop," she called down to her mother. "I'm in bed, Mama. I'm almost asleep. 'Night!"

"Good night," her mother said.

They didn't go in for good-night kisses or being tucked into bed. Only Roderick got good-night kisses or just any-old-time kisses. These would peter off after he stopped being a baby. Once good-night kisses had ended, it would be very hard to begin them again; they would all be too shy to try. Before, when her mother said her own mother had died on Christmas Eve, Marianna had had a feeling of wanting to run to her mother, hold on to her, kiss her cheek. She should have. She should have begun again right then. But she couldn't.

Marianna kept her eyes open as long as she could. The street lamp across the way cast a soft light into her room, and snowflakes reflected on the ceiling made rippling shadows there. Her room looked different in every light, but the things in it were always the same . . . the bed, the chair, the desk, the bureau. Suddenly it struck her that Allie could not look out of a window. "Ah, that would not be very nice," she thought. Finally Marianna went to sleep.

In the morning she could hardly eat her breakfast. At school, in the pageant this morning, she had only two words to say—"A star!"—but she had to say them with wonderment and awe. She practiced saying them so they would not sound the way the teacher said they did in rehearsal. The teacher said they sounded as though she had no soul. Marianna could not help but feel nervous about this.

Nervous or not, she would face the audience, not turn her back on it the way she had one time in room two when she was so scared. And that time she had been standing behind curtains that framed the marionette stage and couldn't even see the audience! But she knew it was there all right, and that the mothers were there, and she turned her back. The curtain did not quite reach the floor, and out front the audience began to guess whose feet were in those shoes that faced backward. They guessed Marianna was standing backward because she was the only one who wore Dr. Scholl's shoes. She had tried to deny it, but no one believed her.

Choking down the last spoonful of oatmeal, Marianna asked her mother if she had a shopping bag to put a present she'd made for Allie McKaye in. Her mother looked at the shoe-box room, and she liked it. She admired it. "That's very pretty," she said, taking in all the details. "Very pretty. Well-built."

"That's a nice little tree in the corner, isn't it? Makes the room look real Christmasy, doesn't it?" Marianna said, as she and her mother lowered the gift carefully into a large A & S shopping bag.

"Oh, come on," her mother said. "I don't want to hear any more about Christmas trees. Is that the mailman I hear out there? I wonder why I don't hear from Frank . . . all this holiday rush . . . I suppose."

It was the mailman, but the children couldn't wait to see if there was a letter from their father or not. While she began to look through the mail, their mother said, "Now remember, today is 'Minnie Day.'"

"Hooray, hooray!" Marianna and Kenny said together. They loved Minnie, and they loved "Minnie Day." Minnie came to clean the house every Friday. It was like having a holiday every single week.

"If I'm not here when you get home this noon," their mother said, "Minnie'll fix sandwiches and soup for you. I promised Josephine I'd mind Silas for her while she went shopping. I'll take Roderick with me. Let's hope he and Silas don't tear each other apart in the pen before she gets back."

Josephine Jimpson was their mother's dearest friend. And their babies had been born on the same day. But that didn't make these babies friends. They threw blocks at each other and grabbed each other's duck or train.

"Does Josephine Jimpson have her tree up yet?" Marianna asked.

"Oh, get off to school, will you? If you need me, remember I'm at the Jimpsons'," their mother said. She didn't sound cross. "Minnie Day" always put everybody in a good mood. "Button up your coats, it's colder out than you think," she said. And off Marianna and Kenny went to school.

They said, "Hi!" to Minnie, who was hurrying up the street, so wrapped up in scarves and coats and a woolen hat you could hardly see her face. A cigarette she was smoking stuck straight out from the folds of her woolen scarves and suggested where her mouth was. She managed to work it to one side of her mouth to speak to them.

"Hi!" she said. "Have a good day, today. Last day . . . right?"

"I have to say, 'A star,' in the play," said Marianna.

"Lord! Lord!" said Minnie. Her cigarette fell out of her mouth then. Kenny picked it up, brushed the snow off and put it back in Minnie's mouth in its original straight-out position. It was still smoking.

"Hurry up, you'll be late," Minnie managed to say.

Marianna gave Minnie a hug. Then she and Kenny hurried up to P.S. 9.

The Tree in a Bottle

THE MINUTE anyone opened the door at P.S. 9, he would know it was Christmas. Smell of pine, sound of carols being rehearsed, pictures on the windowpanes of Santa Claus, wreaths, houses brightly lighted, and angels, children talking out loud and laughing, no one saying, "Be quiet."

Kenny went into his room and Marianna hers, across the hall. Right away Marianna saw that Allie McKaye wasn't there. She was disappointed. Perhaps Allie's barge was not the one with the Christmas tree on deck, tied up at Pier 16. Instead, Allie's barge might have been the one she had seen heading out to sea last night. Now, how could she give Allie the shoe-box room with the bureau in it and the drawers you could pull in and out? And who would say Allie's two words in the pageant—"Look! yonder . . ." Supposing the teacher asked her to say Allie's two words in addition to her own! That would mean she would have to say four words instead of two. Marianna began to feel twice as nervous as before.

But suddenly, panting for breath, Allie arrived, her cheeks bright red. That was a long run from the end of Pier 16 to school!

"Hi!" Marianna said. "I began to be afraid that you weren't coming today, and I had made a Christmas present for you. Here."

"For me?" said Allie.

"Yop," said Marianna. "Take it out of the bag." But Marianna took it out because Allie was too shy to do that. She put the shoe-box room on Allie's desk.

"O-o-oh, how pretty!" said Allie. "Look at the little bureau—and the drawers—they open and close. And handkerchiefs in the little top drawer, all folded up. And a red rug! O-oh! And look at the tree—all decorated . . ." Allie's face glowed. And she began to unbutton her long green coat.

In a very low voice that no one could hear, Marianna said, "Allie is that your **barge that has a Christmas** tree on it, all lighted up, at Pier

16? Kenny and me could just barely see it through the snow last night, and we wondered if it was yours."

"Yes," said Allie. She pursed her lips together and lowered her eyes, not to have to see that someone might have heard. Allie didn't like to say anything about her barge or any barge. So far only the teacher and now Marianna and Kenny knew where she lived. The teacher never brought it up, not even when they were studying different kinds of boats, including tugboats and barges. But Allie was always afraid it would come out that she lived on a barge.

She knew what the others might say if they knew.

They might say, "What is your address?"

"The barge."

"What's its name?"

"The *Anna Maria*."

"Where do you keep it?"

"Pier sixteen."

"Is that all the address you have? The *Anna Maria*, Pier 16?"

No reply.

"Do you sleep in a hammock? Or in a bunk?"

No reply.

"What do you keep your things in—a trunk? A bunk?"

No reply.

"A trunk in a bunk! Ha-ha, ha-ha!"

That's what they had said in the school she used to go to, and Allie didn't want to begin hearing the same old things here. She went into the cloakroom, and Marianna followed her. They were alone there.

"It looked so pretty through the snow, Allie, your barge did, with the tree on it . . ." Marianna said.

"My father put the tree up," Allie said proudly. "It was hard to do—to make it stand up and not blow over. But he did it. He can do anything."

"Just think!" Marianna sighed. "You have a Christmas tree on your barge, and we don't have one in our house where it's easy to have one. Besides, we never have had a Christmas tree in our whole lives, and I am nine." Then, because she didn't want Allie to think she had an awful mother, she added, "Everybody doesn't have to do everything everybody else does . . ."

"That's right," said Allie. "But I bet you will have a Christmas tree this year." Her bright blue eyes sparkled. "Here it is!" She reached her hand into a deep pocket of her long coat. "Be careful of it," she said, handing a small package to Marianna. "It's my present to you!" she said, as they went over to Marianna's desk.

Marianna carefully unwound the paper and opened her gift. It was a little box made of pine wood, and inside, on a piece of white cotton, there was a little glass bottle. Some glass bottles have ships in them. But this bottle had a miniature Christmas tree in it made of glass, its delicate pine needles made of green glass, its trimmings—tiny glass balls of many colors. Glass candles were on the tree, and at the top there was an ornament made of four candles, which, if they were real and lighted, would make two angels go round and round and touch miniature tinkling bells.

Marianna was speechless. Finally she said, "How pretty! I never saw anything so pretty in my whole life. How could they get the tree in the bottle? How, I wonder?"

"My father did it . . . my father made it," said Allie. She was very happy because she could see how enchanted Marianna was.

"He did!" said Marianna. "My! He must be smart. We all—my mother especially—like to make things. But none of us could make a treasure like this! How did he do it?"

"Well, he learned how to blow glass when he was a prisoner in the war long ago. Another prisoner, who said he used to work in a glass factory in Venice, well, he taught my father some of the secrets of glass blowing," said Allie. "My father made me a tree in a bottle last year. This year he made one for you . . . I told him about you, the way we always have lunch together . . ." said Allie.

"Oh, thank you. Oh, please thank him very much," said Marianna. "I'll write him a letter. I'll draw him a picture!" She was overwhelmed. Imagine the captain of a barge, whom she didn't even know, making her this lovely gift! "Now, isn't this funny?" she said. "I made you a room with a bureau in it . . . because you want a bureau . . ."

"Yes," said Allie. "And . . ."

"And . . ." Marianna interrupted. "You—your father—made me a Christmas tree, and that's what I want more than anything else right now . . ."

"But it's glass," said Allie merrily. "Not real . . ."

"And your bureau is cardboard . . . not real either," said Marianna. "Hey! Maybe they mean we really will have . . . me, a Christmas tree and you, a bureau."

"Me, a bureau on land, though," said Allie laughing. "And you, a tree in the house, lighted."

"Oh, yes," said Marianna.

Allie said, "Once I stayed over night at a girl's house, and she had her own room and her own bureau in it. That's the kind of room I'd like, the kind she had. My father and mother used to live in a house, we lived in a house until I was two. I remember it. I think I remember it. Then people tore the house down to make room for a new highway. So my father decided we would live on his barge. My father likes it, and my mother says she does too. So that's where we live, all the time. Between trips and during trips we live on the barge."

"What's the name of it?" asked Marianna.

"The *Anna Maria*," said Allie.

"My name, only backwards," said Marianna.

"Yes," said Allie. "My mother and father thought that was very interesting. We talked about it after dinner last night while my father was finishing your present."

That was all that Marianna and Allie had time to say because right then the teacher said, "Everybody in line."

It was time to go to the assembly hall for the Christmas program, and Marianna, who was to be a shepherd, had to begin to think about the way she would say, "A star!"

Pete Calahan saw her mouthing the words. He opened his mouth, let his jaw hang down, raised his eyes to heaven, and walked solemnly by. He was to be Joseph, being the tallest boy, and he didn't have a worry in his head, because his words were being chanted by the chorus off stage.

It took a long time to get to the assembly hall. On the way each class stopped long enough to peer into every single room to see its Christmas tree because every tree was different. The tree in Kenny's room was

39

decorated with medieval ornaments—princesses in tall pointed hats, unicorns, lutes and other musical instruments, and pieces of colored transparent paper pasted into a mosaic supposed to look like stained glass windows. Kenny had gotten the idea of this tree from the Metropolitan Museum of Art.

"He's as smart as Mama about making things," Marianna thought proudly, because it was the prettiest tree of all the trees so far; and they went on to the next room. "Too bad we don't have earphones," Marianna thought, "the way they do in the museum, to explain each tree when we come to it."

The biggest tree was in the assembly hall and needed no explanation. Every boy and girl in the school had made something for the tree. Marianna couldn't see the Santa Claus she had made, but she did spot Kenny's fish he had pounded out of a tin can. He had stuck a green marble in it for an eye, and his fish hung under a small green light bulb, so it shone all the time and its pink worsted mouth grinned happily.

The program went off without a hitch. Marianna did not stand backward, and she said, "A star!" at the right time. She said it very fast so it sounded like a shooting star. That didn't matter because everybody said their lines very fast, and the program was over almost before it had started, it seemed. Marianna was sorry when it was all over.

She told Mr. Mitchner, the principal of the school who was being Santa Claus, that she thought this was the prettiest Christmas party ever at P.S. 9.

"I think so, too," he said. And he added, "What do you want for Christmas, Marianna?"

"A Christmas tree," she said.

"Oh-ho, oh-ho," said Mr. Mitchner.

Then he said oh-ho, oh-ho to everybody and wished them all a merry Christmas, and they all raced back helter-skelter to their classrooms to get their coats and to start Christmas vacation—a time for no studying, for making presents, and for trimming their own trees at home.

By the time Marianna got back to her classroom, Allie McKaye had disappeared. Her long coat was gone from its hanger, and the A & S shopping bag with the shoe-box bedroom was gone, too. So Marianna left the schoolhouse along with Pete Calahan, as it happened.

"Hi!" she said, and clutched her hat.

Pete didn't answer. He dropped his mouth wide open, rolled his eyes to heaven, and squeaked, "A star!" Then he ran off to Cobble Hill nearby, where he lived.

"No wonder Allie doesn't want that mean old Pete Calahan to know she lives on a barge," Marianna thought, and she started for home alone.

The Christmas-Tree Game

MARIANNA WALKED along slowly. It had stopped snowing, and the snow on the ground was melting in the wan noonday sun. The whistle on the chocolate factory was blowing, so it must be twelve o'clock exactly. It felt funny to be out of school at this early hour instead of at three. Kenny had stayed in school to help dismantle the trees.

Students from the college had put many more trees out by the trash cans. Probably today was the last day of classes for them, too. Some were piling luggage into their little cars or strapping skis on top or behind where they stuck up like antlers. Then they'd start up their little cars with a roar, sounding as though they were going sixty miles a minute, scaring everybody and making the pigeons strut aside in the nick of time.

Marianna lingered beside the discarded trees. In her mind she compared them with the one she had at home. She felt inside her coat pocket for the present Allie had given her—the tree in the bottle. It was her mascot and would give her courage to say, the minute she got home,

"Mama! How about we bring the tree in now so Kenny and me can start trimming it?" Just open her mouth and out the words would come, like this morning, when she'd said, "A star!"

Then she remembered that it was "Minnie Day" and that her mother wasn't home. She knew Minnie wouldn't help her bring the tree in. Minnie knew, the whole block knew—except for old Mrs. Alysius who forgot—that Marianna's mother didn't go in for Christmas trees. They didn't understand it, but they accepted the idea that Marianna's mother had a determination not to be like every tom-dick-and-harry, and they liked her anyway.

Marianna looked up and down the street. There were even more trees for sale today than yesterday. They were leaning against each other, tied up with shaggy hemp rope, beside the stores or clustered around lampposts at the curb. Men were saying, "Buy a tree! Buy your Christmas tree here. More inside. Whassa matter? You don't like this tree? Perfect . . . perfect. Wait, don't go . . . more inside!"

"It all smells just like Maine," Marianna thought. "Like Lebanon, Maine." She knew the smell of pine in Maine, for she had often visited her Aunt Lyddy on her farm. She knew how it felt to walk barefoot on the thick brown carpet of pine needles and sink in where squirrels and chipmunks had tunneled. There were hundreds of Christmas trees on Aunt Lyddy's farm and all around as far as you could see. Marianna's pockets could never hold all the pine cones she picked up that she wanted to take home to her friends in Brooklyn.

Marianna sauntered on. "Oh, pray that Mama hasn't thrown my tree away. Pray that she will let us keep it," she said. She didn't realize that she had spoken out loud, but she had, and someone who suddenly came

running up beside her said, "Oh, she will. Of course, she will."

It was Allie McKaye. Only Allie could have appeared so suddenly from nowhere. Marianna was very happy to see her. "Hi!" she said. "I thought you'd gone home. I looked for you to say good-by."

"I did go home," said Allie. "I ran home with my shoe-box room, and my father and mother loved it. I brought you back your big shopping bag. My mother wants me to go to the store for her and buy some cranberries. She said I could play with you until four o'clock if you want me to."

"That's great," said Marianna. "If you're still at my house when my mother comes home, maybe she will say, 'O.K. Bring in the Yule tree.' She'll mean the tree you saw me bringing home yesterday. It's in the garden."

"Well," Allie said, "if you really think your mother has thrown that tree away, maybe you should bring home another one of those thrown-away trees back there. She wouldn't keep *on* throwing trees away, would she?"

"She might," said Marianna. "She just likes to be different from everybody else. She has a right to be different," she added defensively.

"Oh, sure," said Allie.

"But I . . . Kenny and me . . . we want a Christmas tree, we do," said Marianna.

"Oh, come on then," said Allie. "Let's take home another tree . . . see what happens. She might change her mind."

"O.K.," said Marianna.

They ran back to the houses where most of the discarded trees were. It sounded jolly there—laughter inside the houses, lusty guffaws, voices from the doorways saying, "Have a good time!" "See ya!" "Break a leg."

Marianna and Allie made up a game—the Christmas tree game. Allie was the seller of trees, Marianna the buyer. "Do you like this one?" Allie asked, holding one upright. "Pure spruce from Nova Scotia."

"Hm-m-m," said Marianna, eyeing the tree critically from every side. "Hm-m-m. A little scrawny in the middle there."

Allie laid that tree aside and stood up another one. "Take this one," she said, revolving it slowly. "Thick in the right places, thin in the others. A lady just offered me ten dollars for it! Ten! Yours for the asking . . ."

"Not bad," said Marianna, pursing her lips together, considering it thoughtfully. "H-m-m," she said.

"Make up your mind," said Allie. "But you better take it. This one comes from Lebanon, Maine. The trees there are very fine, very fine . . ."

"Lebanon!" said Marianna. "How do you know about Lebanon? My Aunt Lyddy lives there. I've even been there."

"You have?" said Allie. "Well. I haven't been there, but the cargo we brought in last week was a cargo of Christmas trees that came from Lebanon. They were loaded on our barge in Portsmouth, and the man there said they came from Lebanon, Maine."

Marianna was amazed. "That is funny, isn't it, Allie? That I have visited Lebanon and that the trees you brought came from Lebanon. Wait till I tell that to Kenny!"

Allie nodded. "Yeh," she said. "The tree on our barge is one of those trees from Lebanon. It's a balsam."

"That settles it," said Marianna, getting back to the tree game. "I'll take this tree from Lebanon home. It will make my mother remember Maine," she said.

Allie laughed. "Let's take them all," she said. "We'll hoist this whole batch of cast-away Christmas trees to your house."

"All!" exclaimed Marianna. "I don't think we can keep even one, let alone 'them all.'" But she was already grabbing hold of one to take it home.

"I just know," Allie said, "that when your mother sees all the trees we'll bring home and we tell her they are from Lebanon where your Aunt Lyddy lives, she'll say, 'Well, isn't that nice now? Having a tree from my old home!' And she'll say, she really will say, 'Let's see which one we should keep, take into the house, and trim.'"

"And she'll play the tree game there in the garden with us, choosing the best . . ." Marianna added. "And I hope it will look as pretty in our window as yours does on the barge."

Allie McKaye was no longer shy with Marianna. She talked about the barge and how it put her to sleep at night, rocking against the dock, making the water say, "Slurp . . . slurp . . . . sh-sh. . . ."

"There should be a song about it. *Home, home on the barge*," Marianna said. "Like *Home, home on the range*."

"I did make up a song about the barge," Allie said. "But it's not a happy song. I won't sing it now."

"Oh, dear," said Marianna. "I know it's a sad song. No bureau on the barge. You shouldn't worry so much about not having a bureau."

"It's not only the bureau," said Allie. "It's everything. I want to live like other girls do . . . in a house, not on a barge. Every house that I see . . . I study it. I study it and I think . . . would I like to live in that one? Or this one? Some houses frighten me even more than the barge. But there are other houses, other houses . . . I dream of living in one of those."

"Well," said Marianna. "Some day you will, I bet. And me . . . maybe I shouldn't worry so much about not having a Christmas tree. But I do. So, come on. We'll take this pretty one first, this almost brand-new balsam tree from Maine."

Allie took the trunk end and Marianna the spiky top end, and off they went. "This is much easier than carrying a tree all by myself like I did yesterday," Marianna said. "It's much more fun having company."

"Much 'more better,'" said Allie. *More Better* was the name of the fruit store where Allie was going to buy her cranberries afterwards. Both girls laughed and felt happy.

A boy ran past them. "Tim-ber-r-r!" he screamed. It was Pete Calahan.

Marianna's neighbor, Mrs. Alysius, went hurriedly past them, going the other way, toward the shops. "Bringing home another tree!" she exclaimed.

Marianna laughed. "Yes," she said.

And they trudged along with the tree, and soon they came to Marianna's house with its bright red front door. "Who-oa, Allie," said Marianna. "This is where I live."

"What a pretty house!" Allie said.

"Is it the kind of house you would like to live in if you could choose?" asked Marianna.

"Oh, yes. Oh, my, yes," said Allie. Her eyes shone. "I'm going to pray to live in a house exactly like this," she said. "Every minute I'm going to pray that." Suddenly she became shy again. "I hope your mother won't holler at me because I helped you bring home another Christmas tree," she said.

"Don't worry," said Marianna. "Mama's not home. Anyway, I'm the one to worry, not you."

"Will she hit you?" asked Allie.

"Nope," said Marianna. "She'll just say something like, 'Get those firs out of our yard and be quick about it!'

"Oh," said Allie.

"If Mama comes home while you are still here," Marianna said, "just remember to call the baby 'Roderick,' not 'Baby,' and that will please her very much."

"All right," said Allie.

"Now, come on in," said Marianna. She unlocked the door. "We have to take the tree through the front door and out the back, into the garden. Your end first so we don't break the branches."

The two girls went through the house this way, breaking off only a few small twigs. They stood this new tree beside yesterday's tree. "Still here," said Marianna happily. "Not thrown out."

"A good sign," said Allie. "Your mother didn't throw that tree away, and you may end up having a tree for every room in your house instead of just one tree like everybody else."

Marianna laughed. "Just like P.S. 9," she said. "You should tell Mama that. That would make her real different from everybody else—a tree in every room. Then she still wouldn't be like every tom-dick-and-harry. But come on. We have to get a lot of others. This is fun, isn't it, Allie?"

"Yes," said Allie. "You and me—we're partners. Partners in the Christmas tree business."

They ate the sandwiches that Minnie had made for them. "Never mind the soup," Marianna said. "We don't have time. But before we go, I want to put my present, my glass bottle Christmas tree, in my bureau. Come on upstairs."

"Someone's up there," Allie said, drawing back.

"That's Minnie," said Marianna. "We call Fridays 'Minnie Days.' Hey, Minnie! Hello. We're here."

Minnie came out of one of the back rooms. "I know you're here all right," she said. "I been watching you—first from the front window and then from this here back window. And I sure don't want to be here when your Mama comes home. No sir! I'm leaving early. And you can just tell your Mama that Minnie had to leave early to get her a Chrissus tree for her family. You just tell her that. Hear?"

"O.K.," said Marianna.

She and Allie went up the steep stairway to her bedroom on the third floor. Allie stood in the doorway. "Is this whole room yours?" she asked.

"Yes," said Marianna. She pulled out the top drawer of her bureau, which was painted white, and carefully put her fragile present in it. "See?" she said. "No handkerchiefs. We don't go in for handkerchiefs . . . we just use tissues."

"If I had a bureau," said Allie. "I'd put a stack of white handkerchiefs folded up and ironed into little squares in that top right-hand drawer, the way that girl did in that other house I visited."

"Well, tissues are O.K., said Marianna. "Sanitary . . . no laundering. Look out the window. Do you see that barge down there . . . that barge with the Christmas tree on it, on deck? Is it the *Anna Maria*? Is it?"

"Yes! Why yes, it is!" said Allie. "I never knew you could see it from your house. I never knew anybody could see it from anybody's house. It is my barge. It is the *Anna Maria!* That is our tree on it!"

"From Lebanon . . ." said Marianna. "But come on. We have to hurry. If we're going to have a tree in every room in this house, like in P.S. 9, we have to hurry."

But Allie couldn't tear herself away from the window. "I never saw my barge from away from it, from a house I mean, like this. It looks different . . . smaller . . . pretty, as though it's part of a view. I don't feel as though I belong to it . . ."

"It is pretty," said Marianna. "It's very pretty."

"I know what," said Allie excitedly. "Now that I know which house you live in, we can signal to each other. If your mother lets you keep a —the—tree, one or all of them, but at least one, you can wave a flashlight from the window up here, back and forth, back and forth, over and over. And I will see it, and I will know the good news."

"Hey, yes," said Marianna, excited, too. "Good tidings, good tidings," she hummed. "And if you take off for Buzzards Bay or somewhere, you can get your father to blow seven long blasts on his barge whistle. And I will wave and you will wave. But . . . if Mama doesn't let us keep one of the Christmas trees and put it up and trim it, I'll keep my window dark. I won't turn on the light, not any light."

"O.K.," said Allie cheerfully. "If your light is on, I'll look at you through my binoculars. I'll be standing beside the tree."

"I wish I had binoculars. Kenny and me would look at you back," said Marianna. "But, partner, we just have to hurry, now. Come on."

They tore down the stairs and out the front door. " 'Bye, Minnie!" Marianna called out. "Merry Christmas, if I don't see you again."

"Good-by!" said Minnie. "Merry Christmas! You won't see me again. I'm clearing out of here before your mother comes home, I hope—Lord, Lord!—and sees them firs."

Marianna and Allie brought four more trees home, and then they were tired, and they decided to stop. On the way home with the last one, Mrs. Alysius, on her way back with her shopping cart bulging with groceries, caught up with them. "My!" she said, her face crinkling with a cheerful smile. "That must be a heavy tree if this is all the farther you have come. I'd give you a hand, but I only have two."

"Thanks," said Marianna. "But it isn't heavy."

And Mrs. Alysius, bent over, dragged her heavy cart past them and up the street. "She thinks this is all the same tree," said Marianna, laughing.

"Yes," said Allie. "Now, when we put this tree in the garden, I have to get going, have to get the cranberries."

When they reached the house, Minnie, all bundled up again so all you could see were her eyes and her lighted cigarette sticking through the folds of her woolen scarf, was just coming down the front steps.

She said, "Another tree! Lord, Lord! What you going to do with all those trees? You know your Mama ain't goin' to let you keep one of them . . . no sir . . . not even one of them. I'm getting out of chere before she gets home. Good-by! Br-r-r. It's cold as Janjuary and not even Chrissus yet! Good-by!" This time her cigarette did not fall out.

"Good-by, good-by!" the two girls said. "Merry Christmas!"

Marianna fumbled with the key. Her hands were so cold she could hardly unlock the door. "Come on in and get warmed up. Have some soup before you start for home," Marianna said.

They put the tree out in the garden, and there were six trees now. "It's a forest of fir trees," Marianna said ecstatically. "Just like at Aunt Lyddy's in Lebanon."

Marianna poured out a cup of soup for each of them. They stood at the front window looking out and sipping their soup. Suddenly Marianna exclaimed, "Oh, no, Allie! Will you look at that? That's Kenny coming. And see what *he's* got!"

Kenny was lugging home the hugest tree of all. He waved good-by to someone who must have helped him as far as the corner. Could it have been Mama? Mama had a red coat and so had this person. Marianna ran to the door and opened it, and she and Allie helped Kenny bring his tree in through the house and out into the garden. "Where'd you get this tree?" Marianna asked. "Don't mean to say you met Mama on Atlantic Avenue and she bought it! Is she going to be like every tom-dick-and-harry after all?"

"Oh, no," said Kenny. "This is the assembly hall tree. Mr. Mitchner

53

said I could have it. He helped me home as far as the corner. He still has his Santa Claus suit on. Someone gave us a quarter—she thought Mr. Mitchner was a Salvation Army Santa Claus man. Mr. Mitchner said he was coming my way anyhow because he is being Santa Claus at a church around the corner right now."

"What's he going to do with the quarter?" asked Allie.

"Said he'd give it to the church. The lady who gave it to him disappeared too fast for Mr. Mitchner to explain he was just Mr. Mitchner," said Kenny.

"Gosh!" said Marianna. "But—what a tree!"

"It's a grandfather Christmas tree," said Allie.

"A great-grandfather one," said Marianna.

"An ombudsman," said Kenny laughing, "to keep the other trees calm if they are not chosen. Where'd all the others come from?"

"Me and Allie brought them all home ourselves," said Marianna. "And when Mama comes home, she'll see that we are really determined to have a Christmas tree this year—our first Christmas tree," said Marianna. "She will see we are as determined to have one as she is to not have one."

"Yes," said Kenny.

"We'll stand our ground," said Marianna. "When she comes home, we'll say, 'We have something to show you, Mama . . . it's a surprise.'"

"Put your hands over her eyes," Allie interrupted. "I do that to my ma and pa sometimes."

"Yes?" said Marianna. "Well . . . I don't know about that. But we will lead her into the kitchen—her holding Roderick in her arms—open up the back door . . ."

"... take your hands off her eyes then," said Allie, interrupting again. "Say, 'Surprise!'"

"She'll be surprised all right," said Kenny.

"She already knows about Tree Number One," said Marianna. "I hope she gets home before it's pitch-black night out," said Marianna, "so she can see them all. She might even laugh, make a funny joke—she makes everybody laugh," Marianna explained to Allie. "She's very funny, she makes everybody laugh all the time. She might say, for instance, 'That tree invite in its friends? Creeping Christmas trees! Like creeping lantana.'"

"A disease?" asked Allie.

"No, a flower," said Marianna.

"Oh," said Allie, and gave a polite laugh. "Well, anyway there is supposed to be a moon tonight. And that will make it easier for the *Betsy May,* our tugboat, to shove us out to sea."

"Oh, I hope there will be a moon," said Marianna. "Then we could see you better from the window, and Mama will be able to see the trees if she's real late. But she should be coming any minute."

Allie began to feel shy all over again—you could always tell that because she would always lower her head so her chin practically touched her collar bone. And she jumped every time she heard a step outside. She buttoned up her long green overcoat, pulled her woolen hat down over her ears, put on her bright green mittens, and said, "I'm good and warm now, and I have to go. I can't wait for your mother to come home. So I won't see how surprised she will be or which tree she'll choose or hear her say a funny thing."

"I'll walk you to the store," said Marianna.

"O.K.," said Allie.

" 'Bye, Allie," Kenny said. He kicked his foot against a little yellow carpet-covered hassock, and he said, "I wish some day I . . . we . . . Marianna and me, could visit you on your boat. I mean, you don't *have* to ask us . . ."

Allie didn't answer. She ran out the door. "Wait for me," said Marianna.

As he closed the door behind them, Kenny called out, "Marianna! Don't be long! I'll need you here for when the discovery is made . . ."

"O.K.," said Marianna. "Sweep up the pine needles on the floor while I'm gone!"

Walking Allie Home

MARIANNA AND ALLIE began to run. If you were going along with Allie McKaye, you just had to run. "We had fun, didn't we, Allie?" Marianna panted. "The tree game was fun, wasn't it?"

"Yes," said Allie. "Getting a forest of trees for your garden was fun. If we don't sail tonight, we'll get some more tomorrow," she said.

Marianna laughed and said, "M-m-m," that being all the breath she had left to say.

They turned into Atlantic Avenue. They slowed up to look through the doors of the Syrian shops at the cheeses, olives, bread, baklava, and other sweets. "M-m-m, yummie," said Marianna.

"Let's buy a piece of baklava," said Allie.

"I don't have any money," said Marianna.

"I do," said Allie. "My mother gave me some to buy my lunch. But you gave me my lunch. So . . . now I'll buy the dessert. O.K.?"

"O.K.," said Marianna, and they went into one of the stores, and each of them bought a piece of baklava.

Then, not running now, they sauntered along, and they were finishing their sweets, licking the honey off their fingers, just exactly when
they reached the More Better store. People called the man who ran the
store Mr. More Better. He didn't mind. He took the teasing good-
naturedly and explained every time how the sign painter had left out
the word "and" between "More" and "Better." He didn't want people
to think he was a dope with no education.

More Better was always a pretty store, but it was especially pretty now
with cranberries and red apples, dates, nuts and figs, also holly and red
berries. Over the doorway a sprig of mistletoe was hanging. When Mr.
More Better wasn't warming his hands at the little kerosene stove in
the back of his store and balancing on one foot to warm the other, he
would stand under the mistletoe. He would close his round pale blue
eyes as though expecting a kiss whether the customer were old or young
—a neighborhood joke for the lady customers, some of whom thought
it very funny. Even Marianna's mother, who didn't like Mr. More Better
—she thought he cheated—had stood under the mistletoe for a couple of
minutes, her eyes half-closed, her arms crossed demurely, and a grin on
her face. But Mr. More Better did not kiss her. He gave her a sprig of
holly instead.

Although Mr. More Better didn't kiss anyone who came in or went
out—the mistletoe was all a joke—Marianna and Allie scooted into the
store to buy the cranberries, not taking a chance. It was freezing inside
the store—the kerosene stove didn't do much good with the door wide
open. But Mr. More Better cracked jokes. He didn't complain. He only
complained if you didn't buy a whole lot more fruit and vegetables than
you needed. "Make compotes, make compotes," he'd exclaim bitterly

when you left the mangoes or melons aside.

Marianna felt sorry for Mr. More Better with his rough red hands and swollen feet and all the spoiled fruit he couldn't sell. She wished people wouldn't say he kept his hands on the scale, wouldn't say they thought he cheated, so she could like him without thinking she shouldn't.

Allie McKaye agreed with her. "Even so," she said, "when I buy the cranberries, we will watch the scales and his hands. Because my mother said to."

The two girls did this. They stood, heads together on this side of the scale, and Mr. More Better stood on the other side weighing the berries. His cold hands, almost as red as the cranberries, poised for a second over the scale and then came back down so fast the girls couldn't tell whether he had cheated them or not. They looked at each other. Their eyes agreed that he had not, so they said nothing, and Mr. More Better poured the cranberries into a little brown sack. He gave each of them a large Malaga grape, and they scooted out under the mistletoe.

"He was in the Battle of the Bulge in World War Two," said Marianna, "and his two feet were frozen."

"Oh, my," said Allie. "He should wear fur-lined boots and mittens . . . my father does."

"Oh, poor Mr. More Better! I shall make him a valentine when that day comes, mark it 'from GUESS.' "

"Me, too," said Allie McKaye.

They turned the corner, and now they were at Allie's pier . . . Pier Sixteen. Marianna walked the long length of the pier with Allie. The closer they came to the barge, the more slowly they walked. "She doesn't want to go home," thought Marianna.

The girls were reluctant to say good-by. They stood still and looked about. No one was around. They felt as though they were the only two people alive in the whole world. The sun was setting. The sea was as golden as the sky. Everything was liquid gold and everywhere lights in the city began to come on.

"I love to watch a boat coming under the bridge," said Marianna.

"So do I," said Allie. "Let's wait for one to come . . . unless it's too late for you . . ."

"I'll wait a while," said Marianna. The words were hardly out of her mouth when she exclaimed, "Allie! Look! Look! Something's coming under the bridge . . . it doesn't look like a boat . . . it looks like a house . . . a house floating down the river to the bay! Am I seeing things?"

"It *is* a house," said Allie. "Oh, my! It's a house being moved from somewhere to somewhere else on a barge."

"It's like a dream," said Marianna. "A mirage! A house floating on a sea of gold!"

"It's a real house, that's what it is," said Allie slowly, "a pretty house with a porch on it."

"I didn't know they moved houses on barges," said Marianna.

"My father told me they could do that. But I never saw it done before," said Allie.

"Once I saw a house being moved in Maine," said Marianna, "down a country road. Now it's gotten so they move houses on barges."

Allie was silent. They watched the barge with the house on it until it disappeared from sight around the next wharf.

"Maybe," Marianna said, "maybe some day when your father takes you on a trip, maybe he will have a surprise for you. There will be a house waiting for you somewhere on some other wharf, and your father will have it put on your barge, and he will put it on land somewhere for you to live in. Maybe he will on this very trip . . ."

Allie smiled. "Maybe," she said.

Then they walked over to where Allie's barge was moored and making gulping sounds as the wind and the waves rocked it against the strong old weather-beaten pier. The barge was painted a rich green and its name, the *Anna Maria,* was painted on the sides in bold black letters.

The Christmas tree on its deck was a tall one, and suddenly its lights came on.

Allie jumped aboard. She stood beside the tree a moment. " 'Bye!" she said. "Remember . . . seven whistles mean we are leaving . . ."

"Yes," said Marianna. "And remember . . . my flashlight waving back and forth, back and forth means we have a Christmas tree . . . inside the house and trimmed," said Marianna.

"Yes," said Allie. "Merry Christmas!"

"Merry Christmas!" said Marianna. But Allie had already disappeared down the lighted hatchway.

Good-by, Trees

MARIANNA FELT lonesome. She wished that Allie had asked her to come aboard and had shown her how she lived. She wondered if Allie had a porthole or not and where she did her homework. Allie had told her that the teacher gave her enough homework to last a long time when the *Anna Maria* was going to set out for somewhere. When Allie came back to school, the teacher corrected it. It sounded like fun—doing your homework on a sunny day on deck with sea gulls following behind you, screaming, swooping, swerving, coasting. "Still," she thought, "I might not like that all the time myself. Maybe just once in a while, if the cargo is a pretty one—like Christmas trees."

Pier Sixteen was long. No wonder Allie ran all the time. Marianna felt a little frightened. Twilight was coming, the lights on the bridges and the skyscrapers were coming on, reminding you it was getting late. Dark water could be seen between the heavy planks here and there. She began to run, faster and faster, as fast as Allie McKaye, and she didn't stop running until she got home.

By the time Marianna reached her house, her heart was pounding very fast, not only from running hard, but also from wondering what Mama had said about the trees in the garden. Mama must surely be home by now. She must have said something. Kenny opened the door.

"Well," Marianna asked breathlessly. "Did Mama see the trees? Is she home? What did she say?"

"Well . . ." said Kenny. "I don't know whether she saw them or not. Listen. She came home. From the Jimpsons'. She came through the door, she put Roderick to sleep upstairs. She raced off in the Dodge . . . see? It isn't there. She said she had an errand to do, that J. J.—Josephine Jimpson—had stayed longer than she meant to, said that people ask a favor of you and then they overdo. She asked had any more mail been delivered, and I said no. She said she'd be back soon. Said not to wake the baby, to give him his bottle if he did wake up . . . it's on the stove . . . warming . . ."

Marianna took her coat off and hung it in the closet. There was hardly room for it, there were so many coat hangers in there with nothing on them. She took the extra coat hangers out and put them on the table. They were all green, the color of coat hanger the little lady at the dry cleaners always used. Her mother would be pleased that she had cleared the coat closet without anyone even asking her to.

Marianna joined Kenny at the window. "O-o-oh, Kenny! Look!" she said. "You didn't sweep up very well. Look at all those pine needles!" she scolded. "I'll quick get the broom . . ."

But it was too late. They heard the old gray Dodge. They knew it by the way the brakes screeched. There their mother was, getting out of the car, her arms laden with packages. They opened the door for her, they took some of her packages, and they looked at her face. She looked tired and rather cross.

"Was there another delivery of mail while I was gone?" she asked.

"No, Mama," Kenny said.

"I don't see why I don't get a letter from Frank, he's usually so good about writing. I suppose it's all this avalanche of Christmas cards, and a letter from him is probably sitting right over in the post office—I wish I could go through all that mail myself. I bet we won't hear from Frank until after Christmas ..."

Then she said, "What's all this muss all over Minnie's nice clean floor? All over the front stoop, in the hall, here in the dining room, out into the kitchen. Why'd you track in all this mess especially on 'Minnie Day'?" She followed the trail of pine needles and twigs from the front door to the back.

"Oh, dear, Kenny. You should have swept up better," Marianna said sadly.

"I know it," he said with a sigh.

"Never mind," said Marianna. "It probably wouldn't make any difference. Don't feel bad."

Their mother opened the back door and looked out in the garden. The light from the kitchen and from the dining room windows shone on the trees leaning against the brick wall. "How'd all those trees get out there?" she asked.

Kenny and Marianna went and stood beside her stolidly. "I brought home the big one," said Kenny, "from school."

"I brought all the others," said Marianna. "Allie McKaye helped me. We played a game, the Christmas tree game, and brought them home together."

"Allie McKaye? Who's she?" asked their mother.

"She's the girl I told you about in my class that I made the shoe-box room for—you liked it," said Marianna.

"Where does Allie McKaye live?" asked their mother.

"I already told you," said Marianna. "Allie lives on a barge, the *Anna Maria*. It *is* the barge that has the Christmas tree on deck."

"Well, Christopher Columbus!" their mother said.

"These trees didn't cost anything," said Marianna. "They are as good as new. Allie and me thought you might like to play the tree game, a game we made up. You choose the prettiest one for inside. Or else that we bring them all in and have a tree in every room like in P.S. 9. That would make it that we are not like tom-dick-and-harry . . ."

Their mother didn't answer. Maybe she was pondering this idea. She took off her bright red gloves and scarf. For a person who loved red so much, you would think she'd love to have a tree with dozens of just red ornaments on it. The children waited for her to say something. She said, "Now. Both of you get on your coats and your mittens and take those mangy trees back out. And don't bring any more home. And when you get back, you sweep up all this mess. They're a fire hazard— that's what those dried up old trees out there are. Why, the fellow back of us might throw a lighted cigarette over the wall, and we'd all burn up."

She sounded very tired, her voice was flat, not very angry. It just sounded as though she was surprised at how unreasonable Kenny and Marianna were. She added, "If the baby—Roderick—got some of those pine needles up his nose or down his throat, they might make him choke. He's crawling all over the place now, you know." And she said, "If I told you once, I've told you a million-trillion times, I don't go in for Christmas trees, and I'm not going to begin now. I'm not now or ever going to be like every tom-dick-and-harry."

Neither Marianna nor Kenny tried to be just as determined to stand their ground and have their tree as she was not to have one. They put on their coats and mittens and went out into the garden. A pale moon was rising beyond the trees. It had grown colder and might go down to ten above tonight.

"I knew she'd say that," said Kenny. "I knew it all along."

Marianna didn't answer. Hot tears rolled down her cold cheeks. She wiped them away on the back of her mitten and resolved not to cry, not out loud anyway.

From the bay she heard a muted whistle. It was not a deep-toned whistle, so it could not be from Allie's barge. Now, when she did hear the *Anna Maria* blow its whistle seven long times, if it did sail tonight, she wouldn't be able to signal, "Yes, we have a Christmas tree, we do." She would have to keep her window dark.

They took the great-grandfather tree out first. They brought it in through the back door, through the house, and out the front door. "You might just leave them all over there by that apartment house," their mother said. She closed the doors after them, the back door and the front door, as they went out with each tree, not to freeze out the house. Marianna and Kenny made seven trips with the seven trees—and they were finished.

"Good-by, trees," they said.

When they came back in for good, Kenny got the dustpan and brush and swept up the last traces of their Christmas trees. The house looked as clean as it always did at the end of a "Minnie Day." The only thing to remind anyone of the Christmas trees was the fragrant pine smell lingering in the house.

Marianna sat down at the dining room table. She didn't know what to do. She felt lost without the thought of her Christmas trees. She thought maybe she should go up to her room, not turn on the lights, and watch the view. Maybe she would see the *Anna Maria* with its tree on it. Maybe Allie McKaye would be feeling lonesome, too, and might be standing beside her tree trying to locate exactly where Marianna's window was, so if they did sail she'd spot the flashlight—if it came on.

She watched her mother unpack some of the packages. But some she put in the closet unopened. "Don't look inside of these," she said to

Marianna. They were probably presents for her and Kenny, Marianna thought.

Then her mother said, "Marianna. Would you mind taking that bunch of coat hangers down to the cellar. Thank you for clearing them out of the closet. They're nice fresh ones, and I'll take them to the little cleaning lady on Atlantic Avenue tomorrow."

Marianna gathered up the coat hangers. There were so many she could hardly hold on to them all. Her mother opened the cellar door for her. The coat hangers reminded her of something . . . oh, yes, of what her mother said yesterday—"the whole thing (meaning the tree in the department store) might be made out of coat hangers or some other gol-durn thing."

Marianna laughed, struck by a very funny idea. "Would you close the door after me, Mama," she said. "I'm going to make Christmas presents. So don't anyone come down. They're surprises."

She put the coat hangers on a sturdy work table. Then she turned on every light down there. She loved the cellar, but in the nighttime it was spooky in the corners. Everybody in her family loved the cellar because they all liked to make things, to use tools, to paint. Probably Roderick would too when he grew older. Or, he might become an orator when he grew up, the way he liked to carry on monologues—what he said in his language seeming persuasive and sensible if only you knew what it was about.

Marianna sat down on a work bench. She picked up two or three coat hangers and studied them, and she laughed again. "Tree?" she said. "Tree? Christmas tree? Skinny in the right parts, fat in the right parts. Just right."

The Coat-Hanger Christmas Tree

AND NOW, Kenny didn't know what to do. He decided to go up to Marianna's room and look out the window. He was upset. He had never really thought that his mother would say, "O.K. Let's have a tree." But Marianna had gradually seemed to become so sure, she had almost convinced him . . . she and that Allie McKaye with their Christmas tree game. He couldn't stand the idea of Marianna's disappointment. "She was stupid," he thought, "to have had any such idea."

Before going upstairs he went to the cellar door and listened. She might be crying down there all by herself. He put his ear against the door. He didn't hear any crying, though. He just heard clinking, tingling noises, whatever they were—something she was making for somebody for Christmas. So he went upstairs, and he didn't turn on the light, and he looked out.

Kenny could see all the Christmas trees, there where he and Marianna had put them, stacked neatly near the lamppost. "I know what I'll do," he said. "I'll bring one back. When everybody is asleep, in the middle

of the night I'll go out and bring one back for Marianna. I'll trim it,
and I'll tell Mama Santa Claus did it. When they come down in the
morning, there the tree will be at the middle front window, all
trimmed, all lighted, as though brought by Santa Claus—that's the
kind of tree Marianna always wanted most of all, the kind that comes
as by magic in the night. I'll stay up til 2 A.M. to do it. Never you mind,
Marianna. Don't you cry . . . But how can I get the lights, I don't have
any . . . Shucks, ah shucks!"

He watched the view for a long while. But he couldn't get Marianna
out of his mind. He looked at the *Anna Maria,* he could tell it easily in

the dark by the tree, and he thought he saw a tugboat edging up beside her. He couldn't be certain, but it might be, and Marianna wouldn't want to miss seeing Allie's barge sail away. He decided to go downstairs, open the cellar door a crack, and tell her Allie's barge might be getting ready to leave.

Downstairs, his mother was looking out the front window, hoping the postman would make one more late delivery; but she didn't see any sign of him and went to the kitchen to get the baby's bottle. Kenny pressed his ear against the cellar door again. He still heard some clinking sounds, and he heard Marianna chuckling. Then he heard her coming up the stairs, carefully, not two at a time as usual.

"Open the door, somebody," she called up. "O-o-ops!" she said. "Hurry up. Kenny, are you there? Open up."

Kenny opened the door wide.

"Clear the way . . ." said Marianna. "Make way, make way," she said, and she came into the kitchen with—something—in her two hands. She was leaning backward not to bump against it. "Merry Christmas!" she said merrily. "Make way for the first Christmas tree in the house of the Lambs of nine Pine Street."

Kenny and his mother stepped back.

"Behold . . . a tree!" said Marianna. She said it with expression as she had that morning said, "A star!"

"Is that . . . a . . . Christmas tree?" asked Kenny.

"Of course, it's a tree, you dummy," said Marianna, laughing. "What's the matter with your eyes?"

She walked carefully, carefully into the dining room. "Watch out," she said. "Don't bump into me . . . my tree might fall apart." She walked past Roderick, who began an animated explanation, and she put her tree on a small table in front of the middle window in the living room.

"Well," her mother said. "Well, what a tree!" she said, standing back and taking it in.

What a tree it was, indeed! Marianna had made a Christmas tree out of the green coat hangers. She had made it in the exact shape of a Christmas tree. She had wired the coat hanger branches to a curtain rod that was the trunk. She had found a square board for the base and had hammered a thick long nail through the middle of it. The hollow curtain rod fitted over this sturdy nail, holding the coat-hanger Christmas tree upright and quite steady. She had bent the handle of the top coat hanger so it would look like wings of a bird or an angel. The knob at the top of the coat hanger could be supposed to be a head.

"That's some tree you made!" her mother said approvingly. She examined it carefully, and she laughed and said it was quite ingenious. "I couldn't have done better myself," she said.

"Too bad I don't have any lights," Marianna said apologetically. "It would look 'more better' if there were lights . . ."

"Well," her mother said. "I bought a set of lights today for Josephine, she had forgotten them. You can have these lights, and she can get herself another string tomorrow. But that tree! It's really neat, it's great! I can't wait for everybody to see it . . ."

Marianna wound the string of colored lights through the branches. Now and then she stood back, cocked her head, looked at her tree this way and that, studying it, improving it, and then she was satisfied. The coat hangers swayed a little when anyone took a step. But it was sturdy

and did not fall apart.

"Don't anyone breathe too hard," her mother said gaily.

"Kenny, turn the lights on, now. Will you?" Marianna said.

Kenny put in the plug, and the coat-hanger Christmas tree was "on."

Marianna put a little red chair that she was getting too big for in front of the tree, and she sat down in it and she turned the lights on and off, on and off . . .

"Our first Christmas tree," said Kenny dully.

But Roderick, from his little perch exclaimed in ecstasy. He kept reaching his hands toward the lights, and he made explanations in varied tones of voice, giving a long and vivid speech. He pounded the table with his fists and declaimed ardently in his colorful language. He made everybody laugh. Marianna kept clicking the lights on and off and on and off for they were not the self-twinkling kind. Scarcely pausing for breath, Roderick went on and on with his animated conversation, which was so funny everybody laughed until they cried. "O-o-oh!" they gasped. "Roderick, you love the tree so?" and this sent him into further variations.

After a while the laughter subsided. Kenny looked at Marianna soberly. She was still smiling. Her wide eyes were bright and sparkling. From where he was standing Kenny could see the lights of the coat-hanger tree reflected in them.

"Sh-sh-sh," said Marianna, though Kenny had not said a word. "Sh-sh-sh," she said. "If you look at the coat-hanger tree and don't wink . . . just don't wink, you can, if you stare hard enough see a real Christmas tree with balls and tinsel and painted walnuts . . . everything. Just don't blink and you can see it all . . . a beautiful tree."

Kenny blinked.

Marianna looked up at him. "You blinked," she said reproachfully. She looked back at the tree and turned it quickly on and off, on and off again. "It stays in your eyes, if you don't blink. Whatever you want to see here stays in your eyes and in your mind, like the last thing you see in your room, when you switch off your light, well, that thing will stay in your eyes and just gradually fade away in the darkness under your eyelids."

"M-m-m," said Kenny, not blinking.

There was a silence, even Roderick paused for breath.

"I had a lot of fun making this tree," Marianna said. "And, Mama, you love it. I know you love it. It's not a tom-dick-and-harry Christmas tree, this tree isn't . . ."

The front doorbell rang. "Maybe *that's* the mailman," their mother said. But it wasn't. It was her friend Josephine. "Come on in, Josephine," she said. "Look what we've got! See our tree!" she said.

"Your tree!" said Josephine Jimpson. "You mean to say you have turned into one of us?"

Marianna's mother gave a short laugh. "You ought to know me better than that," she said. And she led the way into the living room where Marianna was still sitting and switching the lights on and off and where Roderick was still stretching out his arms and continuing with his orations.

"Oh, no," said Josephine. "A coat-hanger Christmas tree! Now that is brilliant!"

"Marianna made it. She loves it. She can't tear herself away from it, we all love it," said their mother. "And look at Roderick, or rather

listen to him! The tree has inspired him to give a marathon speech."
They all began to laugh again.

Then Josephine became grave. "Hm-hm," she said. "Maybe some time, next Christmas maybe, you might try a real tree . . ." She spoke in a very low tone as though wanting it to seem she might or might not have said anything. It would be up to Marianna's mother to hear or not hear, as she wanted.

Marianna sighed. She stood up and turned on the overhead light. She stretched herself. She left the Christmas lights on for Roderick, but since no one was blinking them any more his talk became low and serious. You could plainly see that the tree was a coat-hanger tree.

Mrs. Jimpson said, "Hm-hm . . . well . . ." again. Sometimes by merely clearing her throat Josephine Jimpson implied as much as a long comment would.

Suddenly, Marianna heard the long drawn-out blast of a boat whistle. "Come on, Kenny," she screamed. She flew to her bedroom two steps at a time. "Come on, Kenny!" They raced to her window where Marianna had a big flashlight ready. "It's Allie's barge!" she said. "She's signaling us. It's the *Anna Maria*!"

They crouched on the floor and stared at Pier Sixteen. "Yes," Marianna said. "Yes, it is! There's a tugboat pushing her out!"

The barge blew again as it straightened out in the bay . . . seven long deep-toned blasts. It sounded almost like the Queen Elizabeth. Marianna thought she saw someone standing by the lighted Christmas tree. "That must be Allie," she said. "She's waiting, watching for my signal. They must be leaving this very minute. Oh! I have to signal—did we or didn't we have a Christmas tree?"

She hesitated only a second. Then she turned her flashlight on, and she waved it back and forth, back and forth until the barge had disappeared. That meant that yes, Marianna did have a Christmas tree.

Because . . . a coat-hanger Christmas tree is a Christmas tree, isn't it?